A NOTE TO PARENTS

When your children are ready to "step into reading," giving them the right books is as crucial as giving them the right food to eat. **Step into Reading Books** present exciting stories and information reinforced with lively, colorful illustrations that make learning to read fun, satisfying, and worthwhile. They are priced so that acquiring an entire library of them is affordable. And they are beginning readers with a difference—they're written on five levels.

Early Step into Reading Books are designed for brand-new readers, with large type and only one or two lines of very simple text per page. **Step 1 Books** feature the same easy-to-read type as the Early Step into Reading Books, but with more words per page. **Step 2 Books** are both longer and slightly more difficult, while **Step 3 Books** introduce readers to paragraphs and fully developed plot lines. **Step 4 Books** offer exciting nonfiction for the increasingly independent reader.

The grade levels assigned to the five steps—preschool through kindergarten for the Early Books, preschool through grade 1 for Step 1, grades 1 through 3 for Step 2, grades 2 through 3 for Step 3, and grades 2 through 4 for Step 4—are intended only as guides. Some children move through all five steps very rapidly; others climb the steps over a period of several years. Either way, these books will help your child "step into reading" in style!

For Daniel

—*S.K.*

To Joe,
my son and buddy

—*J.M.*

Random House 🏠 New York

Text copyright © 2001 by Stephen Krensky
Illustrations copyright © 2001 by Joe Mathieu
All rights reserved under International and Pan-American Copyright Conventions.
Published in the United States by Random House, Inc., New York, and simultaneously
in Canada by Random House of Canada Limited, Toronto.

www.randomhouse.com/kids

Library of Congress Cataloging-in-Publication Data
Krensky, Stephen.
What a mess! / by Stephen Krensky ; illustrated by Joe Mathieu.
p.   cm. — (Step into reading. Step 1 book)
SUMMARY: Although each child is making a mess of his or her own, they
all deny responsibility for the mud being tracked through the house.
ISBN 0-375-80220-7 (trade) — ISBN 0-375-90220-1 (lib. bdg.)
[1. Cleanliness—Fiction. 2. Mud—Fiction.]
I. Mathieu, Joseph, ill.   II. Title.   III. Series.
PZ7.K883 Wem   2001   [E]—dc21   00-032346
Printed in the United States of America   March 2001   10 9 8 7 6 5 4 3 2

STEP INTO READING, RANDOM HOUSE, and the Random House colophon are registered
trademarks and the Step into Reading colophon is a trademark of Random House, Inc.

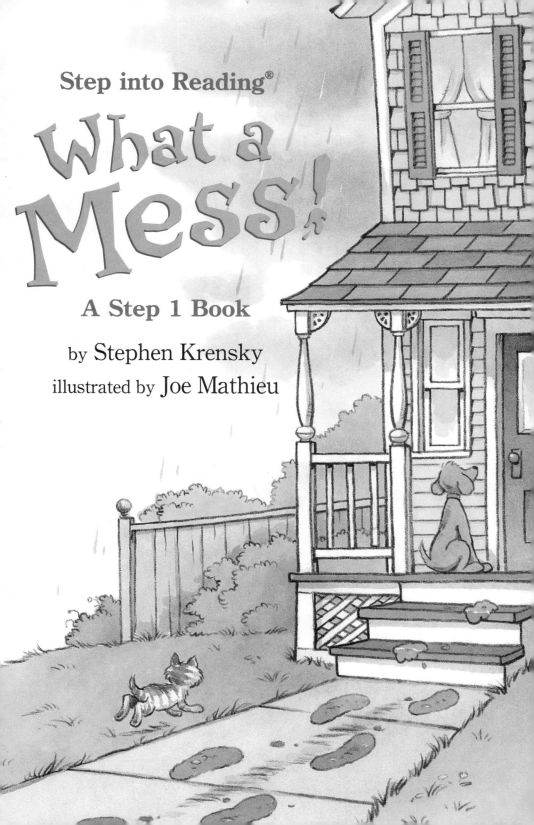

Step into Reading®

What a Mess!

A Step 1 Book

by Stephen Krensky

illustrated by Joe Mathieu

Uh-oh!

Look at the mud.

Mud on the rug.

Who did that?
Who can it be?

"Not me," says Alice.

6

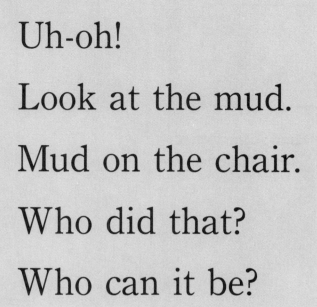

Uh-oh!
Look at the mud.
Mud on the chair.
Who did that?
Who can it be?

"Not me," says Ben.

Uh-oh!
Look at the mud.
Mud in the hall.
Who did that?
Who can it be?

"Not me," says Dennis.

15

Uh-oh!

Look at the mud.

Mud on the stair.

Who did that?

Who can it be?

"Not me," says Ellen.

Uh-oh!

Look at the mud.

Mud on the bed.

Who did that?

Who can it be?

"Not me," says Sarah.

Uh-oh!

Look at the mud.

24

Mud on the sink.

Who did that?

Who can it be?

"Not me," says Lee.

There is mud
on the rug
and mud
on the chair.

Mud in the hall.

And mud
on the stair.

Mud on the bed.

And mud
on the sink.

There is mud
from the rug
all the way
to the tub.
Oh, what a mess!
Mom will be mad—

at Dad!